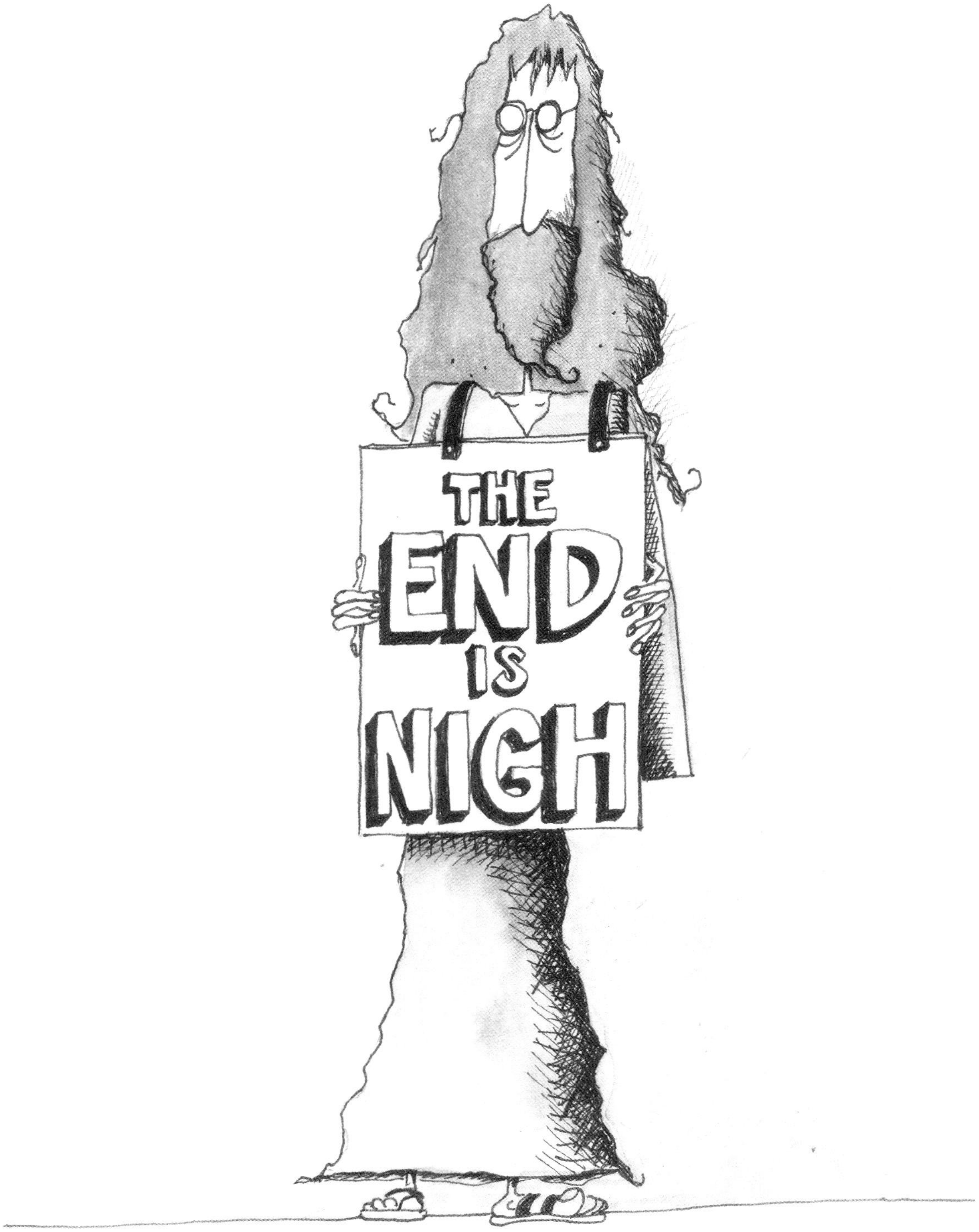
THE
END
IS
NIGH

Another Fine Mess

Another Fine Mess

Peculiar and Amusing Ways to Die

Annie West

NEW ISLAND

ANOTHER FINE MESS
First published in 2018 by
New Island Books
16 Priory Hall Office Park
Stillorgan
County Dublin
Republic of Ireland

www.newisland.ie

Print ISBN: 978-1-84840-705-3

British Library Cataloguing Data.

A CIP catalogue record for this book is available from the British Library.

Typeset by JVR Creative India
Cover design by
Printed by

New Island Books is a member of Publishing Ireland.

'Either he's dead, or my watch has stopped.'
Groucho Marx

'It's funny the way most people love the dead. Once you are dead, you are made for life.'

Jimi Hendrix

Introduction

Death. The only certain thing in life.

One minute you're carefree and risky and silly, jumping off rocks and flinging yourself in harm's way with cheerful abandon because you're young and you'll live forever.

In what appears to be an actual blink of an eye, you wake up and find you're halfway through your life already and the kids are dropping hints about The Will.

When you were young you got a pain in your head. Now you're older you get a pain in your head and immediately assume you're about to die of a massive brain bleed.

Often while out walking in the crisp bright morning you start thinking not just about your own inevitable demise but the manner of your dispatch. Some never think about it but others think about it a lot, often to the point of obsession. Not quite Cotard's syndrome (where sufferers walk around thinking they are, in fact, already dead) but close enough. Others refuse to even discuss the D word in case it somehow hastens the inevitable, or worse, jinxes it.

As a cartoonist and illustrator, naturally I lean towards the more amusing methods of meeting one's end. Struck by lightning (with light-up skeleton effect), maybe a grand piano falling from a tall building. Anything from Roadrunner cartoons. Definitely the way I want to go.

With this in mind, I started looking at interesting and amusing deaths in history. I didn't expect to find much material but was pleasantly surprised. After extensive research, fuelled with pots of carcinogenically strong coffee and artery-clogging cake, I decided to share some of the more amusing ones (I inexplicably came across more than one historical death caused by rubbish jokes about animals eating figs). Of particular interest were fictional deaths inflicted on certain writers who ruined the social lives of Leaving Cert teenagers. I admit I spent many days sitting in Irish class writing lists of Ways to Kill Peig Sayers. Willy Yeats was of course subjected to a variety of tortures. Added to this, I have drawn some ironic (and of course completely exaggerated and fictitious) ways people from history *might* have died.

I also ruminated extensively about the last moments before death. What if they had been portentous, ironic and gruesomely amusing? If not, then let us make them so.

In this book I also express my deep and abiding obsession with people being eaten by huge monsters. I don't know where this came from, or if it's relevant, but it's fun to do.

At the back of this book we've left a page for you to decide and make a note of (or draw) the ideal manner of your own demise. For the record, as it were.

Might be fun for the great grandkids to read in years to come.

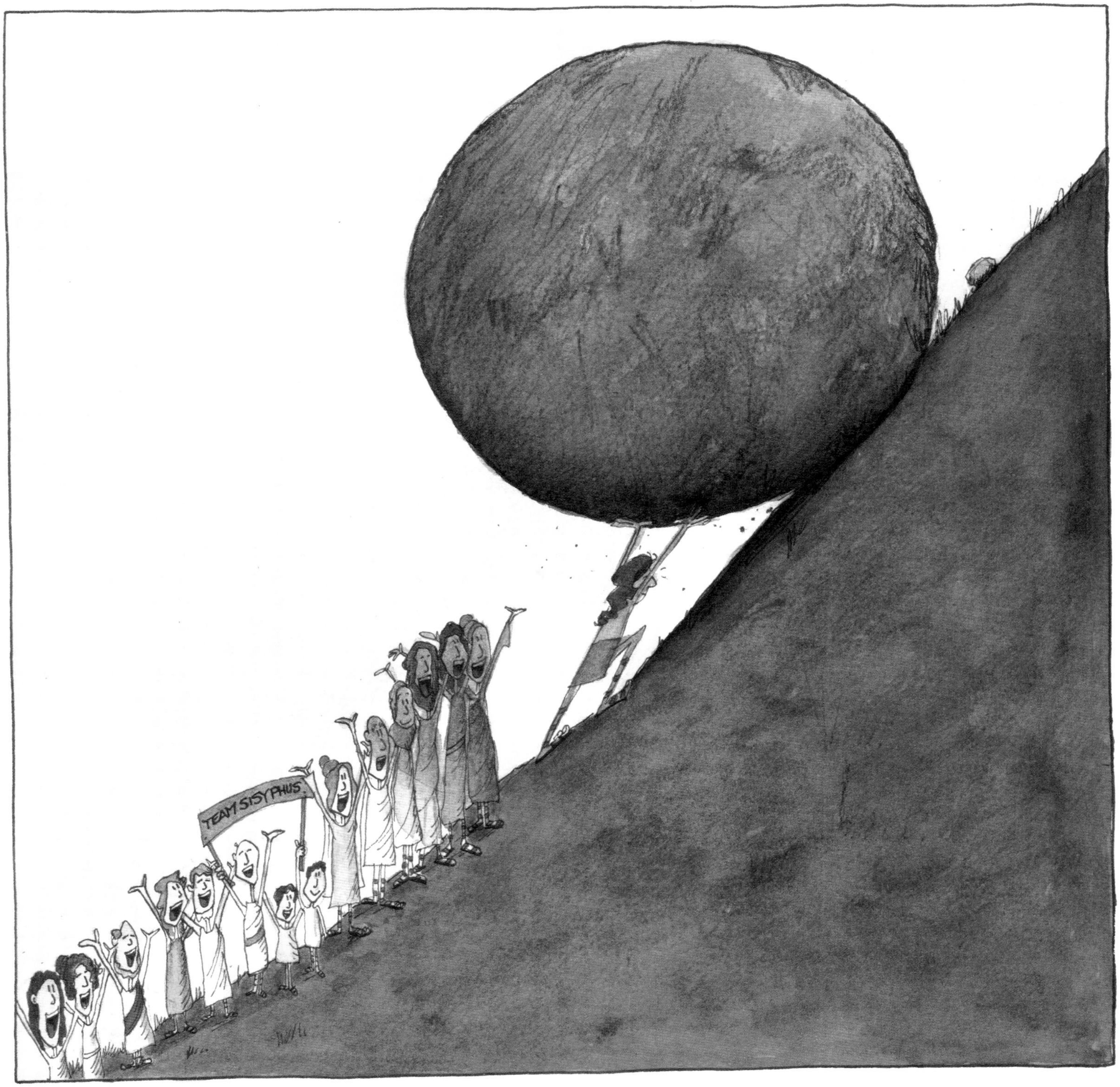
TEAM SISYPHUS

"Come on, Sisyphus! You can do it!"

Hard cheese

Queen Maeve of Connacht – warrior, serial monogamist and alleged murderess of many, including her sister Clothru – occasionally took some time off from murdering and pillaging to bathe in Lough Ree.

Her bereaved and enraged nephew, Furbaide, son of Clothru, decided to even the score and avenge his poor dead mother. He practiced with his slingshot for weeks and eventually dispatched Maeve to her eternal reward, mid-swim, with a well-aimed lump of hard cheese.

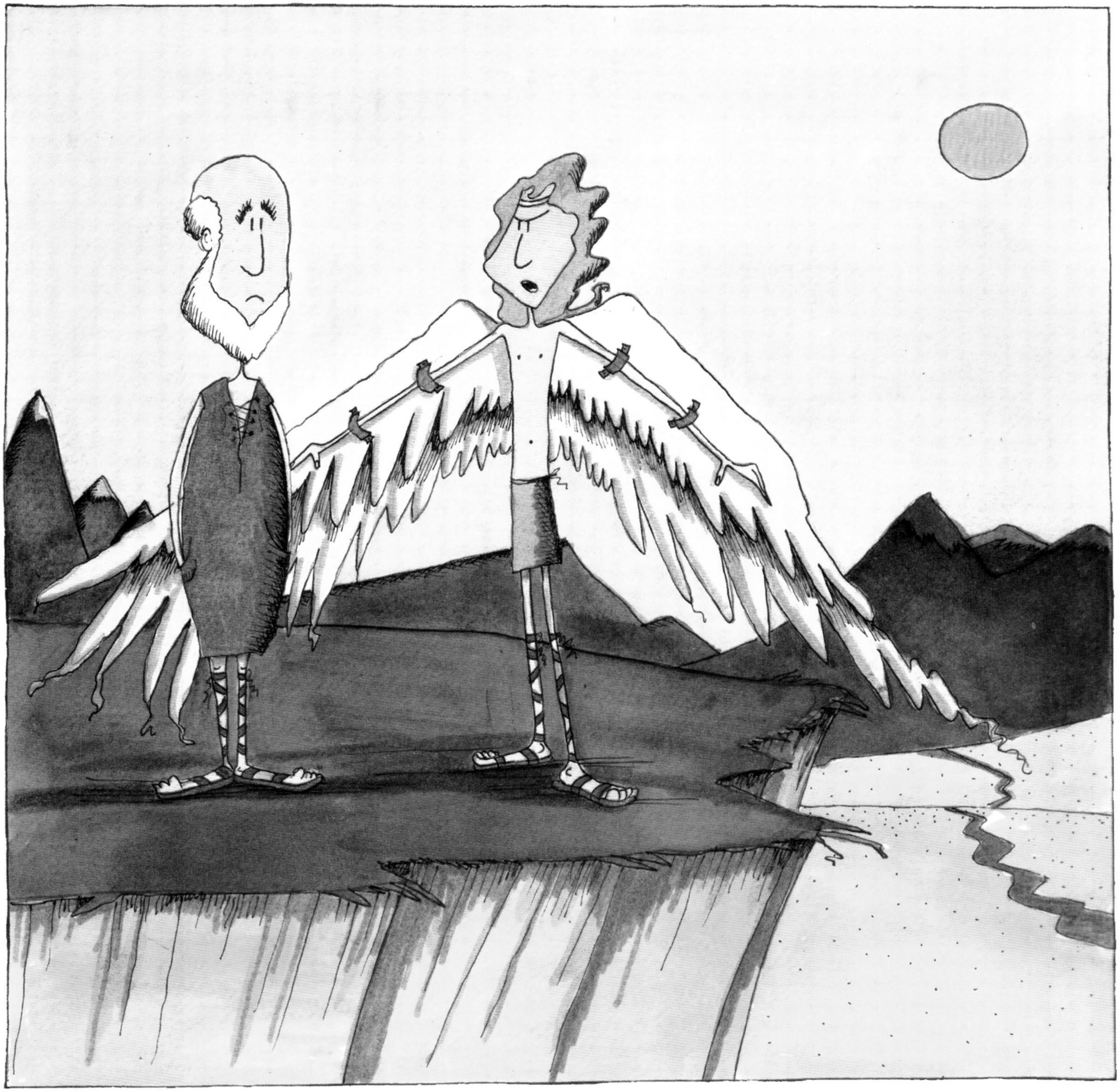

"Stop nagging, Dad. I know what I'm doing."

Anyone seen Draco?

In 600 BC, Athenian lawmaker Draco went to the theatre where many hundreds of supporters and well-wishers arrived to show their appreciation for his leadership, despite his now-legendary introduction of severe penalties for lawbreaking.

An Athenian custom to show respect was to throw cloaks or hats on the person. However, the crowd was so huge and so many people threw their cloaks on Draco that he was eventually buried under a mountain of garments and smothered to death.

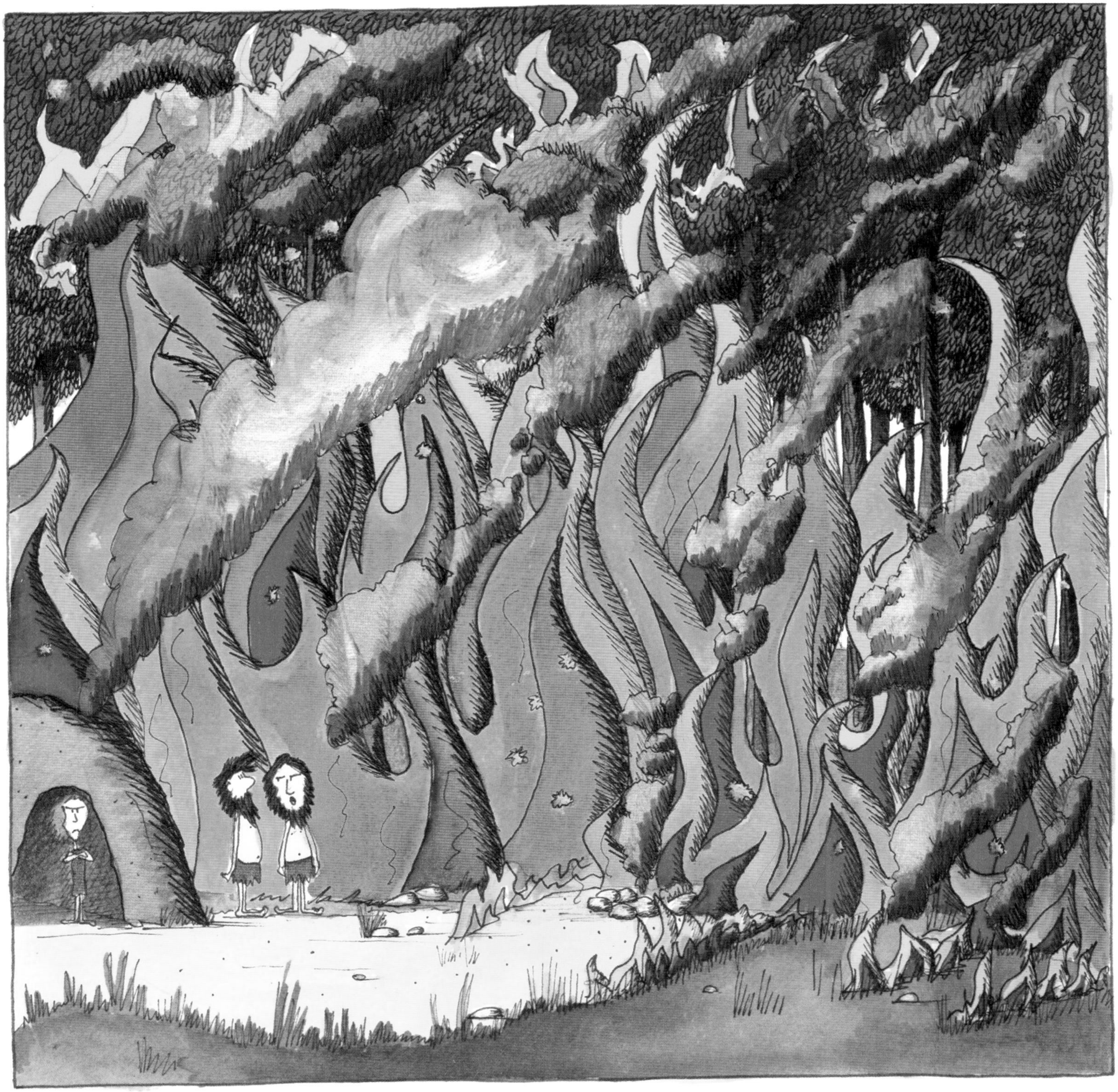

"Okay, you've invented fire. How do you make it stop?"

Hey fellas I think I'm cured

Around 475 BC, the Greek philosopher Heraclitus is said to have been devoured by dogs after going into a cowshed and smearing himself with manure to cure his dropsy.

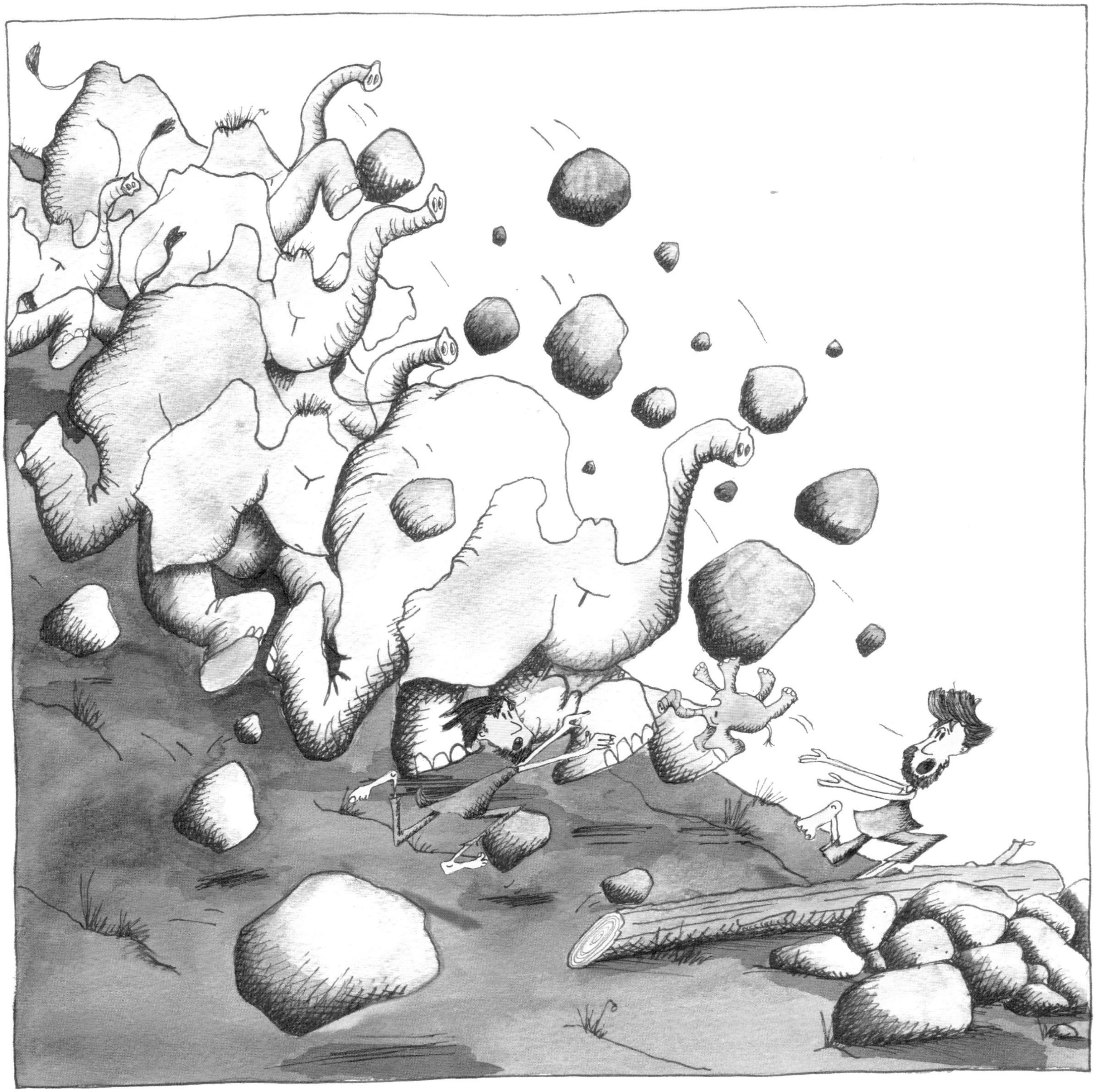

Rugby was first invented in the stone age but nobody ever got to hear about it.

I got this sudden, severe headache out of nowhere

In 456 BC, Aeschylus, the Greek playwright, was killed by a plummeting tortoise. An eagle had dropped it on him, mistaking his bald head for a rock suitable for shattering the reptile's shell.

Ironically, Aeschylus had been staying outdoors because he'd heard a prophecy that he would be killed by a falling object.

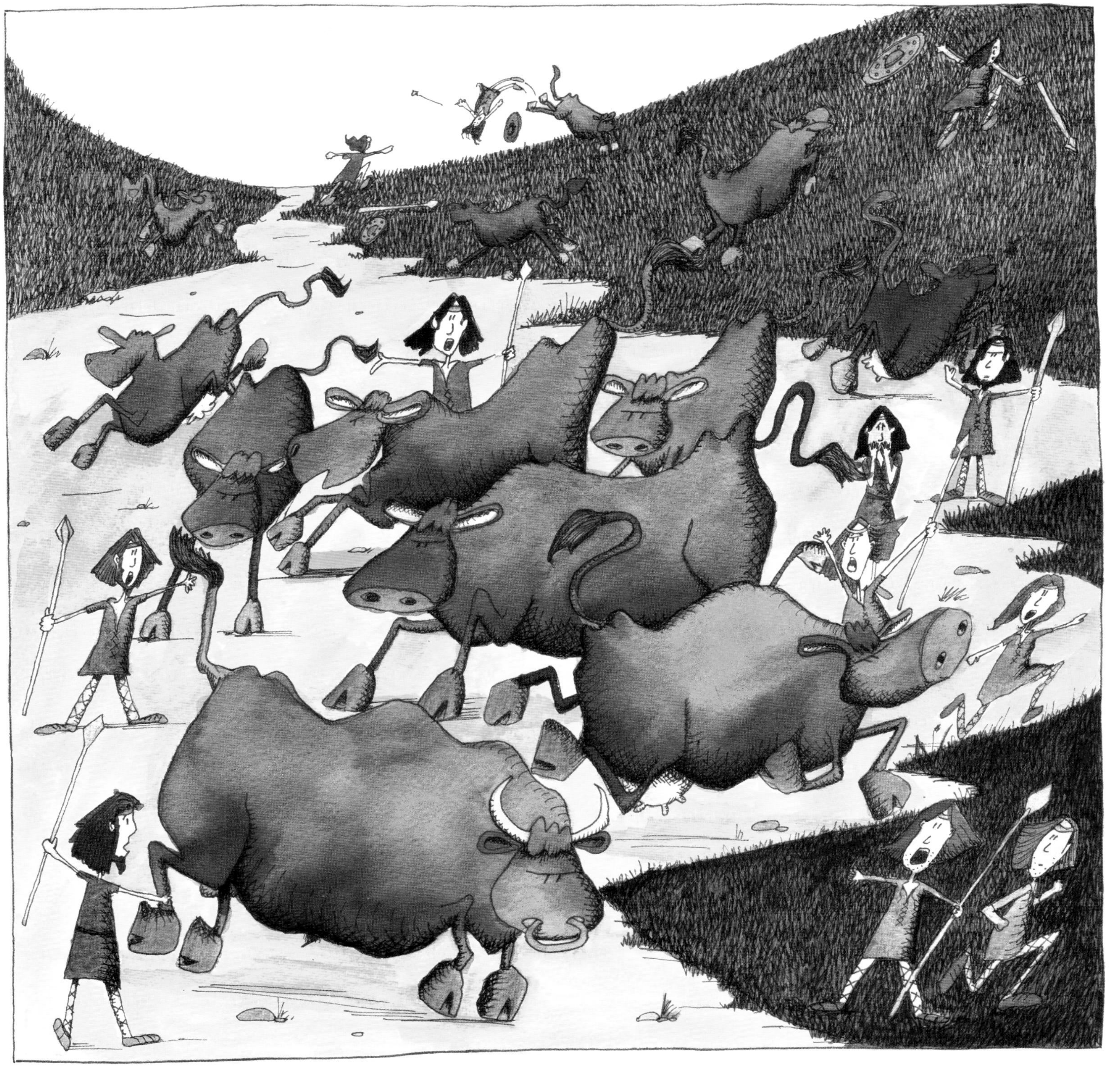

The Cattle Raid of Cooley. Not as easy as it sounds.

There their

In or around the year 285 BC, Philitas of Cos, a Greek intellectual, was said to have become so focused on arguments and correct word usage that he wasted away and starved to death.

So Philitas died from an eating disorder or wasting disease. In other words, one might say he died of pedantry.

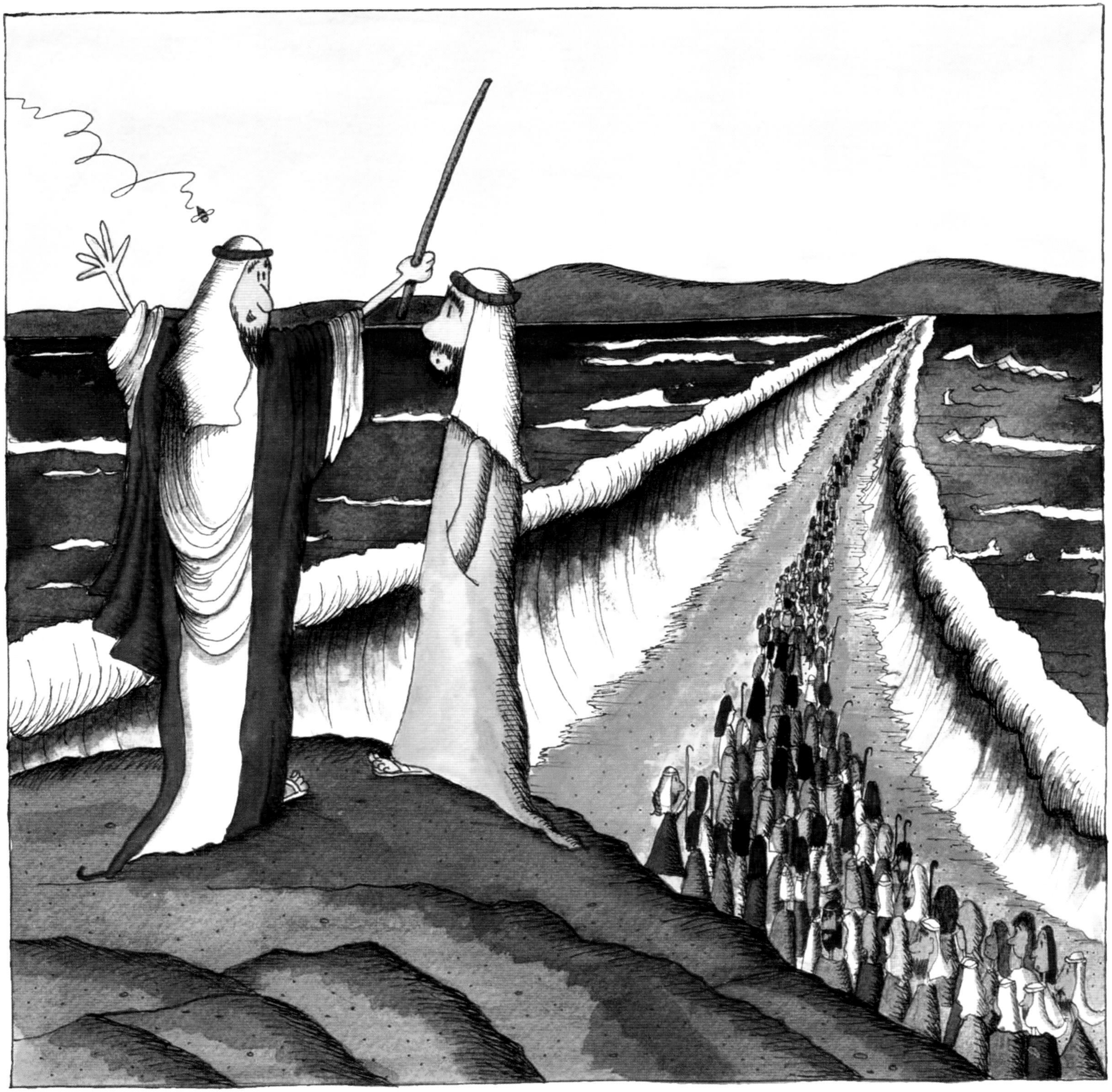

"Oh no it's fine. Just as long as I keep my arms in the air like this."

u ok hun?

One of history's most brilliant tacticians, warlords and all-round villains, Attila the Hun, married a young girl named Ildico in 453 AD. At the wedding banquet he gorged on food and drink. Sometime later, his nose started to bleed. Too drunk to notice, it continued to bleed, and continued to bleed some more, eventually drowning him in his own blood.

When his death was announced, the men of his army, hysterical with grief, cut their long hair and slashed their cheeks.

Attila was buried in three coffins, one nested inside the other like a Russian doll. The outer one was made of iron, the middle one silver, and the inner one was made of gold. According to legend, there was some pretty bad news for the gravediggers: when Attila's body was buried, they were murdered so the grave would never be found.

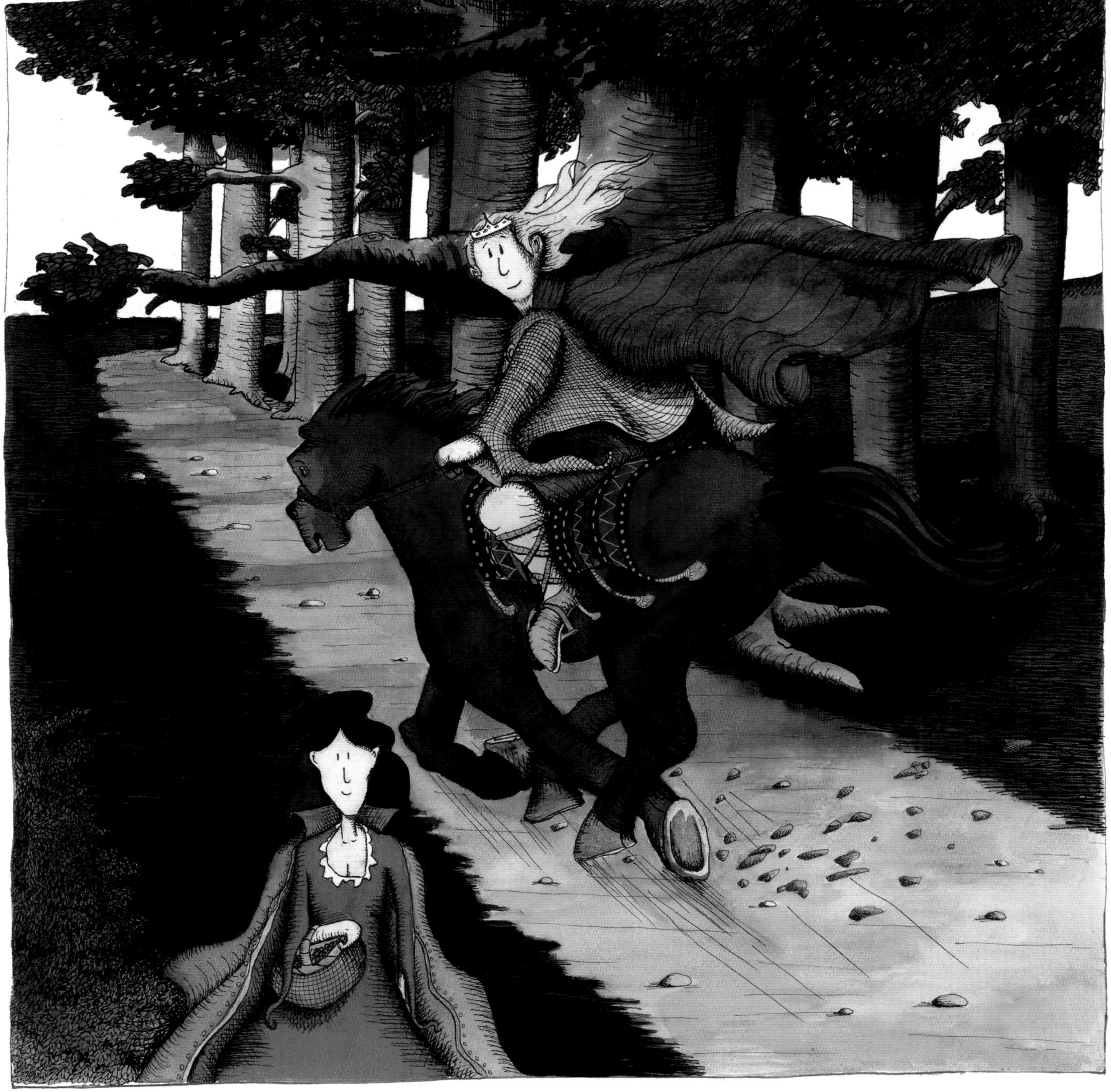

Strongbow forgets warning about being distracted by pretty girls.

I'm here all week, try the veal

Saint Lawrence was one of the seven deacons of the city of Rome in the third century AD. In 258 AD, having insulted the Prefect of Rome by being sarcastic about what actually constituted 'the wonderous riches of God', had both his arms dislocated, was strapped to a huge griddle and roasted alive over what may have been the first barbeque during the persecution of Valerian.

The Christian poet Aurelius Clemens Prudentius wrote that he joked with his torturers: 'Turn me over – I'm done on this side'. He is now the patron saint of cooks, comedians, and firefighters.

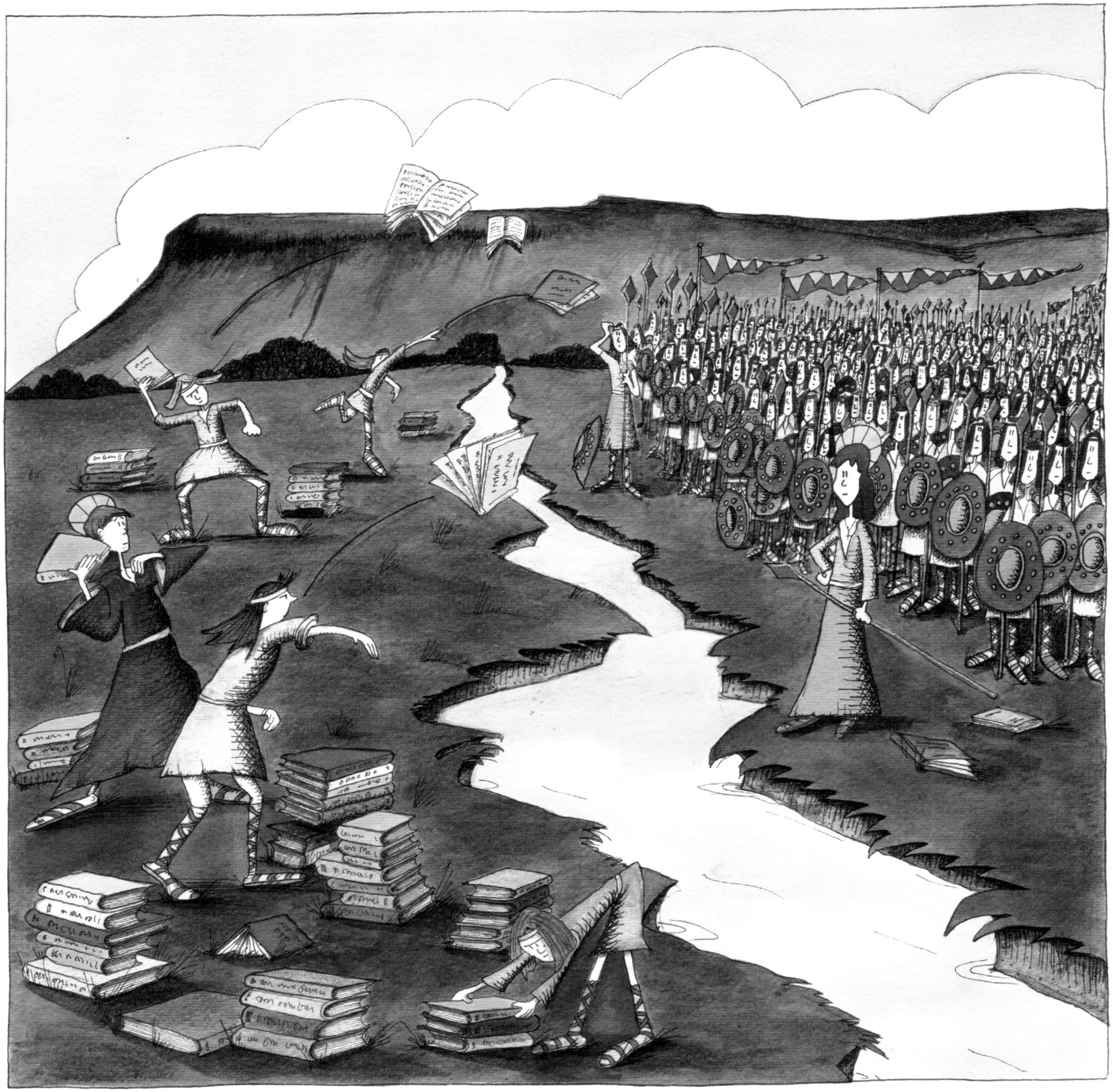

A misunderstanding leads to an early win for St Columba at The Battle of the Books.

Dancing in the moonlight

There is a fanciful belief regarding the death of Li Bai, the greatest and most prolific poet of the Tang Dynasty, which is also known as the Golden Age of Chinese poetry. It is said that in 762 Li Bai drowned after falling from his boat when he tried to embrace the moon (or the reflection of it at any rate) in the Yangtze River. Some would argue that the actual cause of death was too much drink, but the more poetic legend, as it were, has lived on.

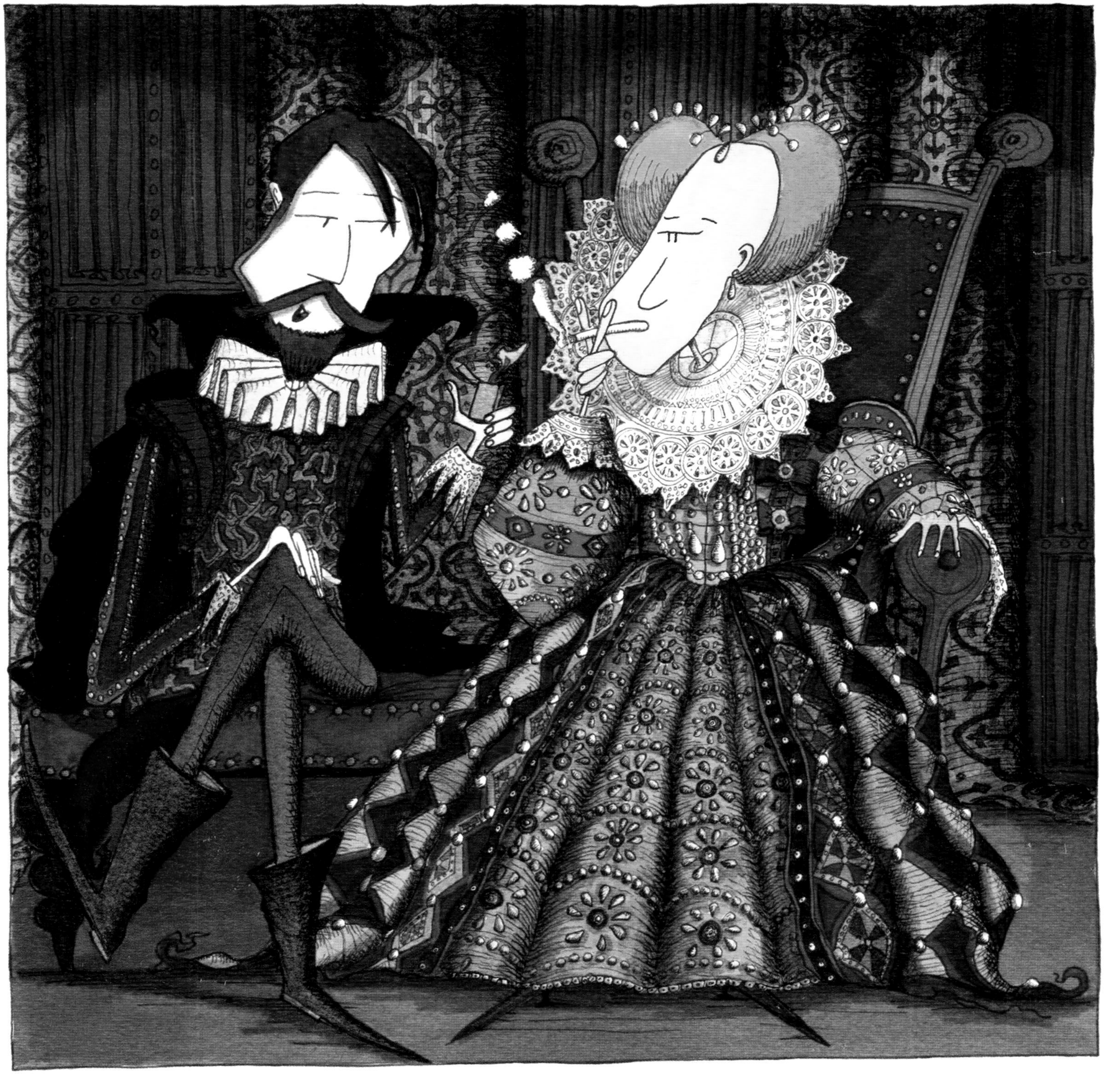

"Oh no it's fine. You can give it up any time you want."

The meteoric rise of Wan Hu

The world's first attempt at space travel allegedly took place as early as 2000 BC during the Ming Dynasty.

Wan Hu, a Chinese official, marked his entry into history books, folk tales and obituaries at the same exact moment.

Wan had decided to take advantage of China's huge advancements in chemistry and rocket technology to launch himself into outer space. Wan set about making history by having a special chair built with forty-seven rockets attached. On the day of lift-off, Wan, wearing beautiful silk ceremonial robes, sat on his rocket chair. Forty-seven servants lit the fuses, and then ran like hell. There was a huge explosion. When the smoke cleared, both Wan and the chair were gone, never to be seen again.

A crater on the moon has been named after him.

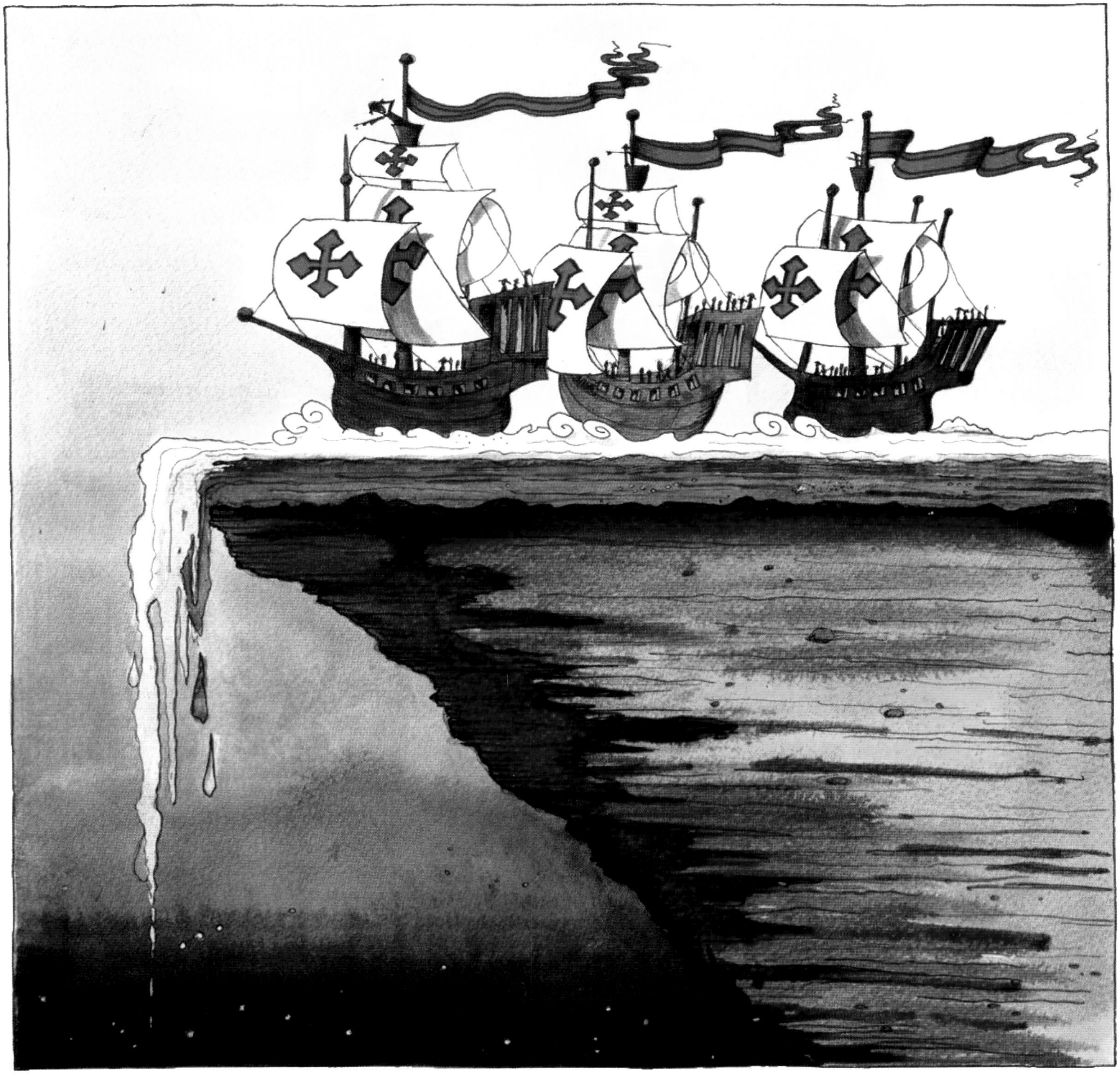

Just then, Columbus realises Aristotle was wrong.

Oh sh**

In 1131, the young King Philip of France died when his horse stumbled over a black pig that had darted out of a dung heap in Paris.

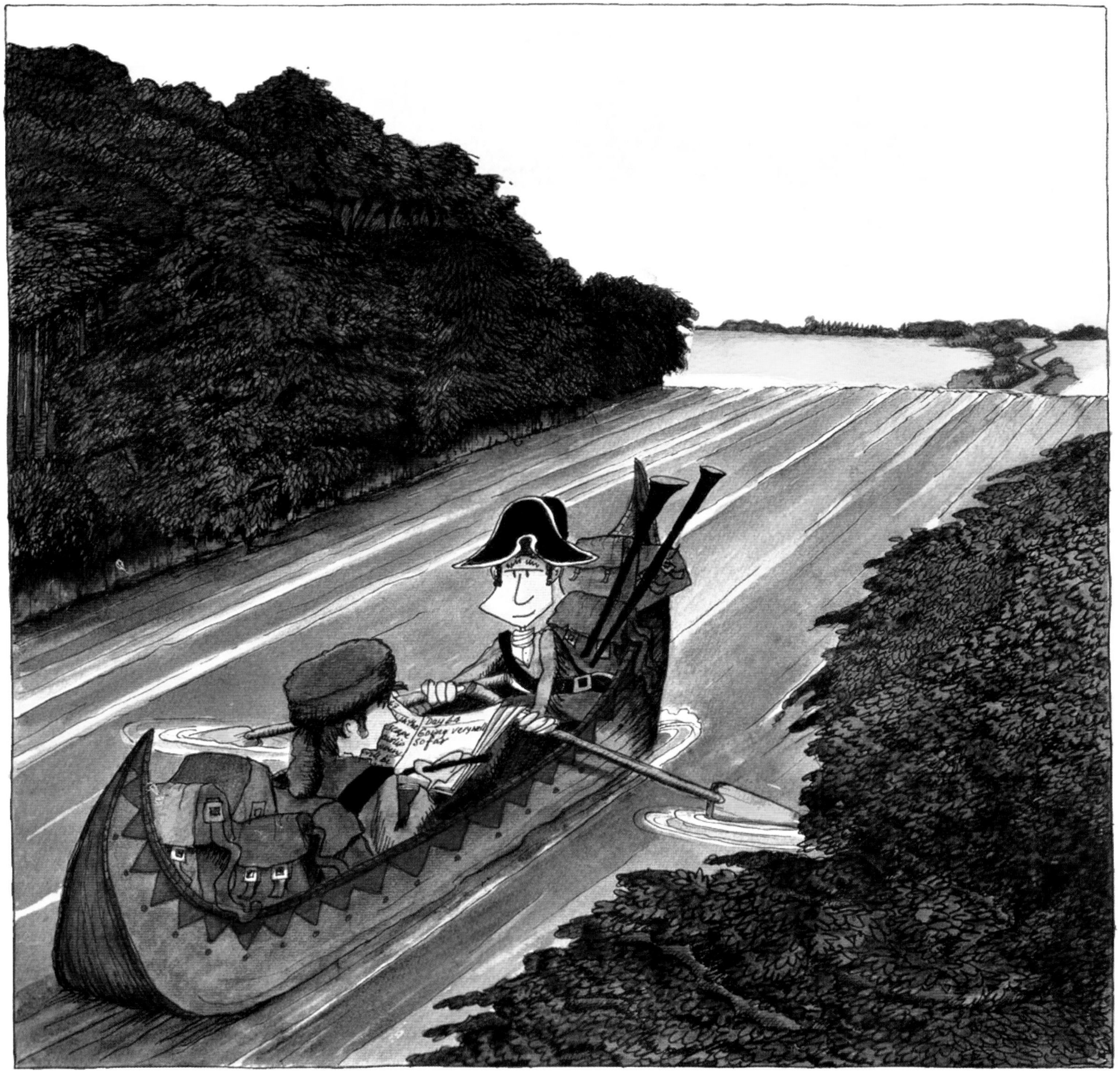
Day 64
Going very well
so far

Dear Mr President,
The expedition is going really well.
Kind regards,
Lewis and Clark

Bal des Ardents

In 1393, a masquerade ball was held at the French royal court to celebrate the marriage of one of the queen's ladies-in-waiting. The young King Charles VI and five of his companions performed a dance as 'wild men', in costumes made from cotton and a sticky and highly combustible resin.

Later that evening, the Duke of Orléans arrived carrying a flaming torch. Leaning in to inspect the dancers' costumes, the duke set the costumes alight, and the dancers' flammable costumes soon became engulfed in flames.

Luckily, the king was saved when his plucky teenaged aunt threw her skirts over him to put out the fire. Another dancer leapt into a vat of wine.

The other four performers were less fortunate, being burned alive, and the whole event became known as the 'Bal des Ardents', or 'Ball of the Burning Men'.

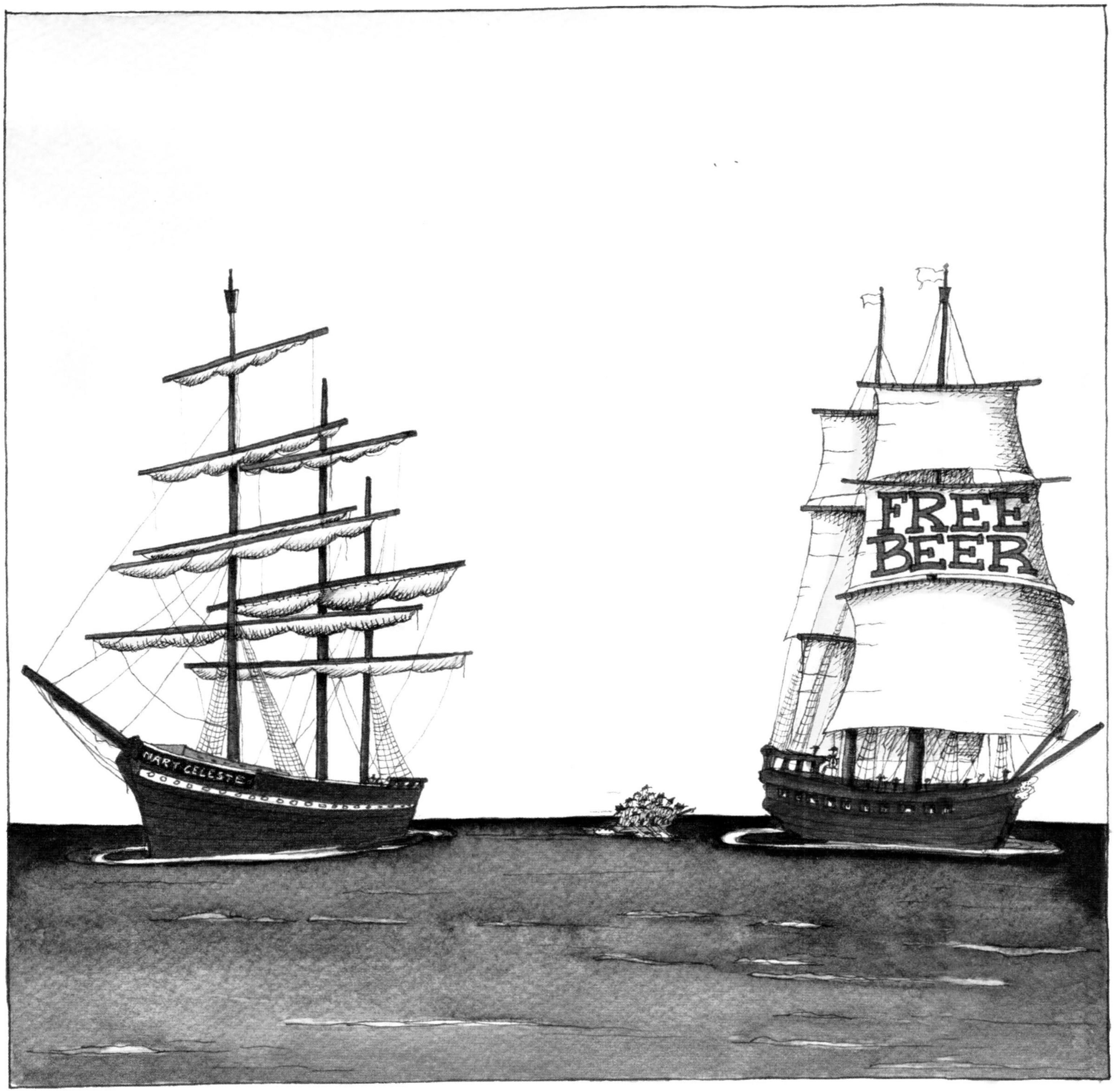
MARY CELESTE
FREE BEER

What really happened.

What a killer joke

In 1410, Martin the Humane, King of Aragon, Valencia, Corsica and Sardinia, died from a combination of indigestion and uncontrollable laughing. According to reports, Martin was suffering from indigestion on account of eating an entire goose in one sitting when his favourite jester, Borra, entered the room. When Martin asked Borra where he had been, the jester replied: 'Out of the next vineyard, where I saw a young deer hanging by his tail from a tree, as if someone had so punished him for stealing figs.'* This joke, though not hugely funny, caused the king to laugh so hard he keeled over and died.

*Interestingly, a very similar, and similarly not very funny, 'Donkey eating Figs' gag also killed Cryssipus, a third century BC Greek Stoic philosopher.

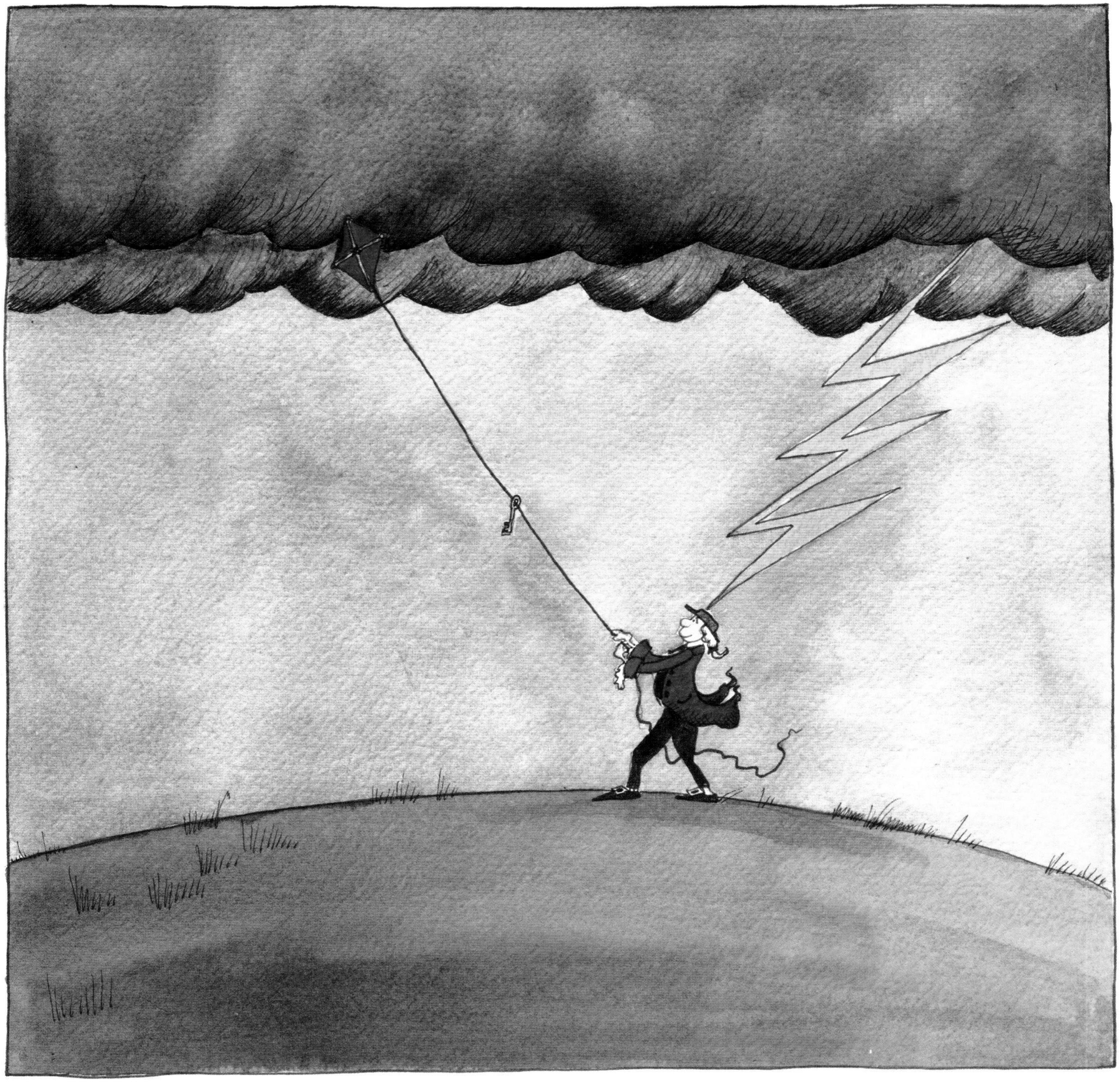

Benjamin Franklin finally gets his kite in the air.

Health & Safety

In 1567, Hans Steininger, the popular mayor of Braunau am Inn, Austria, died when he broke his neck by tripping over his own beard. The beard, which was 4.5ft (1.4m) long at the time, was usually kept rolled up and stuffed in a pocket – but a large fire broke out in the town and while helping to put the fire out he was seen running around with it hanging free. In the midst of the commotion he managed to step on his own beard, sending him tumbling down a flight of stairs where he broke his neck.

Visitors to the town can see the 450-year-old beard (minus its owner), chemically preserved in a glass case in the District Museum Herzogsburg in Branau.

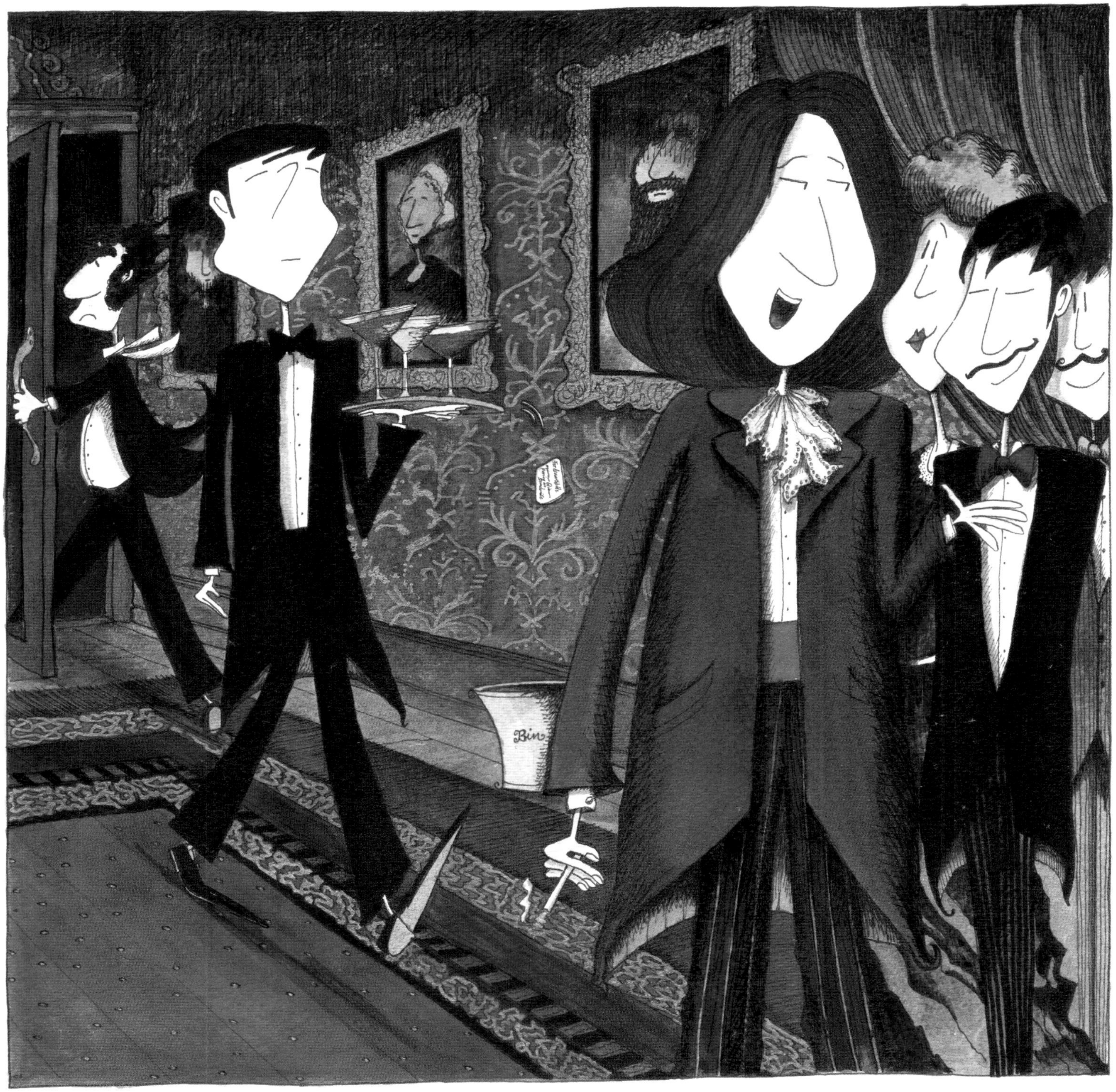
Bin

A tiny gust of wind could have saved Oscar Wilde from a slow and painful death.

The king who ate himself to death

In 1771, Adolf Frederick, King of Sweden, died of digestion problems shortly after finishing a meal of lobster, caviar, sauerkraut, smoked herring, kippers and champagne, topped off with fourteen servings of his favourite dessert – a soft milk brioche filled with whipped cream and almond paste, served in a bowl of hot milk, called *hetvägg*.

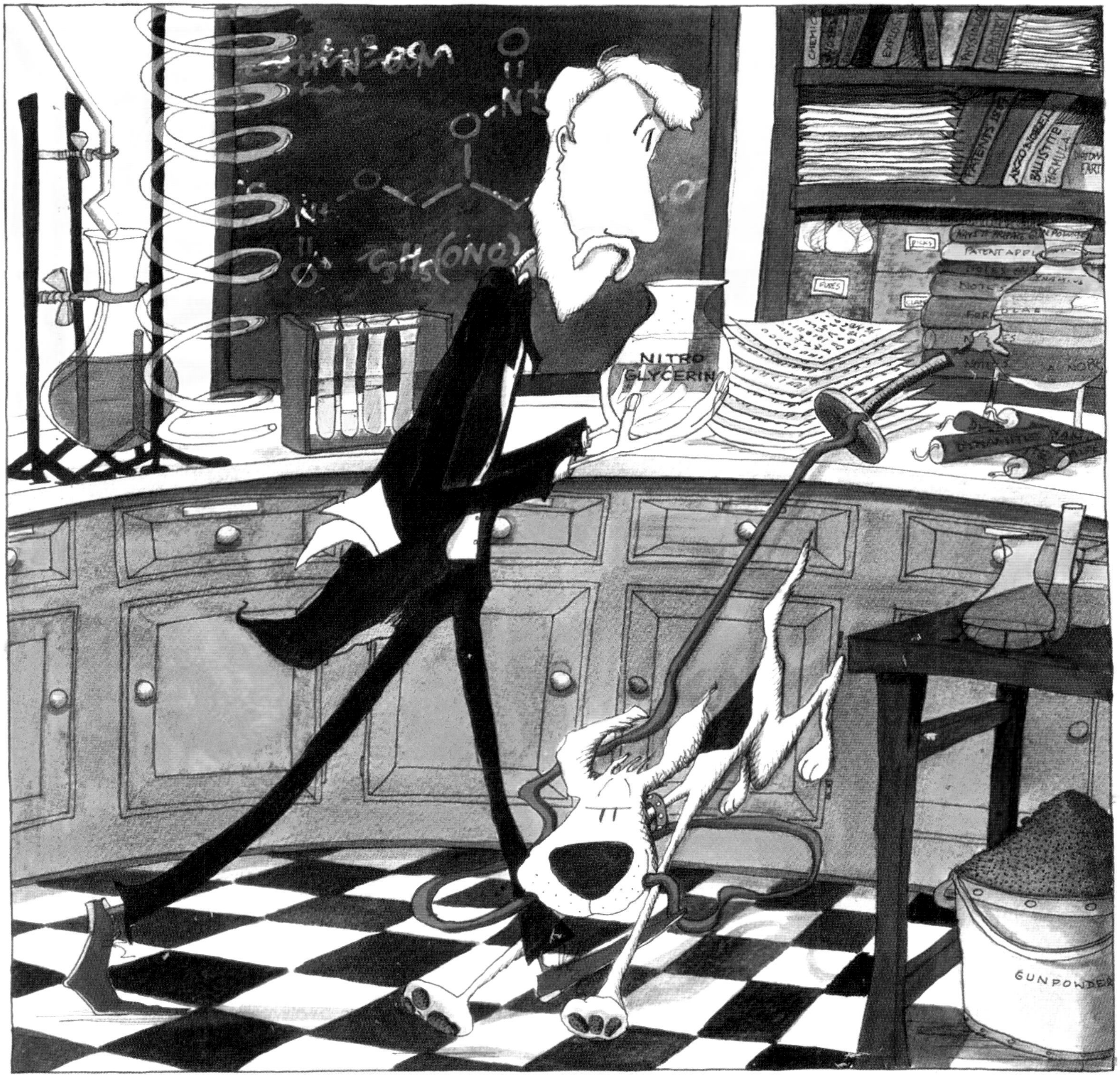
NITRO
GLYCERIN
GUNPOWDER

Alfred Nobel rarely observed health and safety recommendations.

Skin deep

During the seventeenth and eighteenth centuries, it was fashionable for ladies to have pale white skin and red rouged cheeks. They used lead-based Venetian ceruse as a foundation for their make-up. The noxious effects of the lead contained therein caused hideous skin eruptions, which the ladies, most notably the beautiful but rather vain Maria, Countess of Coventry, then covered up with more toxic foundation, which in turn eventually led to blood poisoning, which killed Maria on 30 September 1760 at the age of twenty-seven.

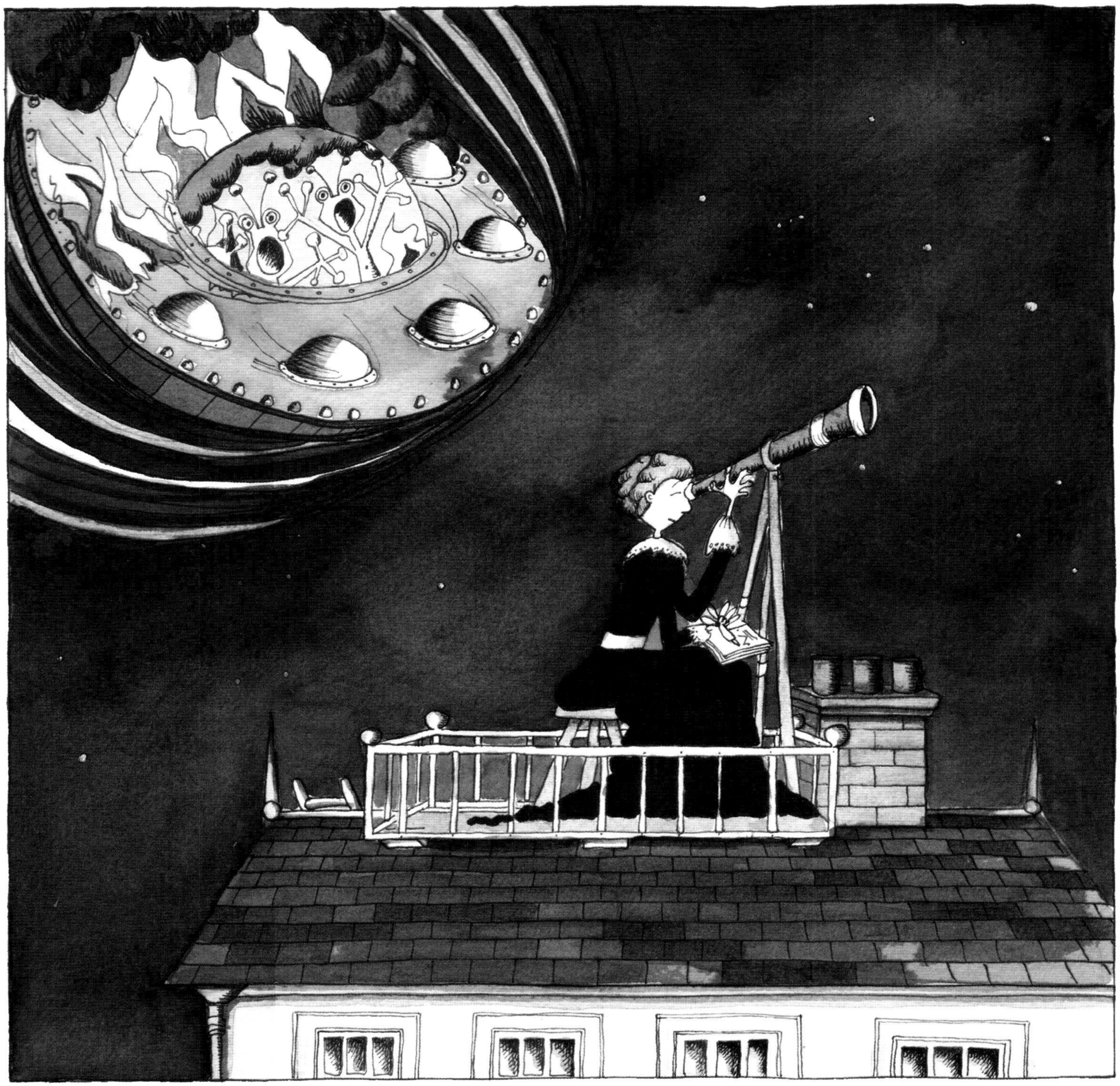

Astronomer Maria Mitchell observes an amazing new faraway star.

Case dismissed

Clement Laird Vallandigham, a lawyer and politician from Ohio, was in court defending a man on a charge of murder. He was demonstrating to the court with a supposedly unloaded gun how the victim might have accidentally shot himself while in the process of drawing his gun on the night in question. As it happened, the gun was in fact loaded and the lawyer shot himself in the kidney.

Vallandigham's unfortunate and ultimately fatal demonstration proved his point, and the defendant, Thomas McGehan, was acquitted.

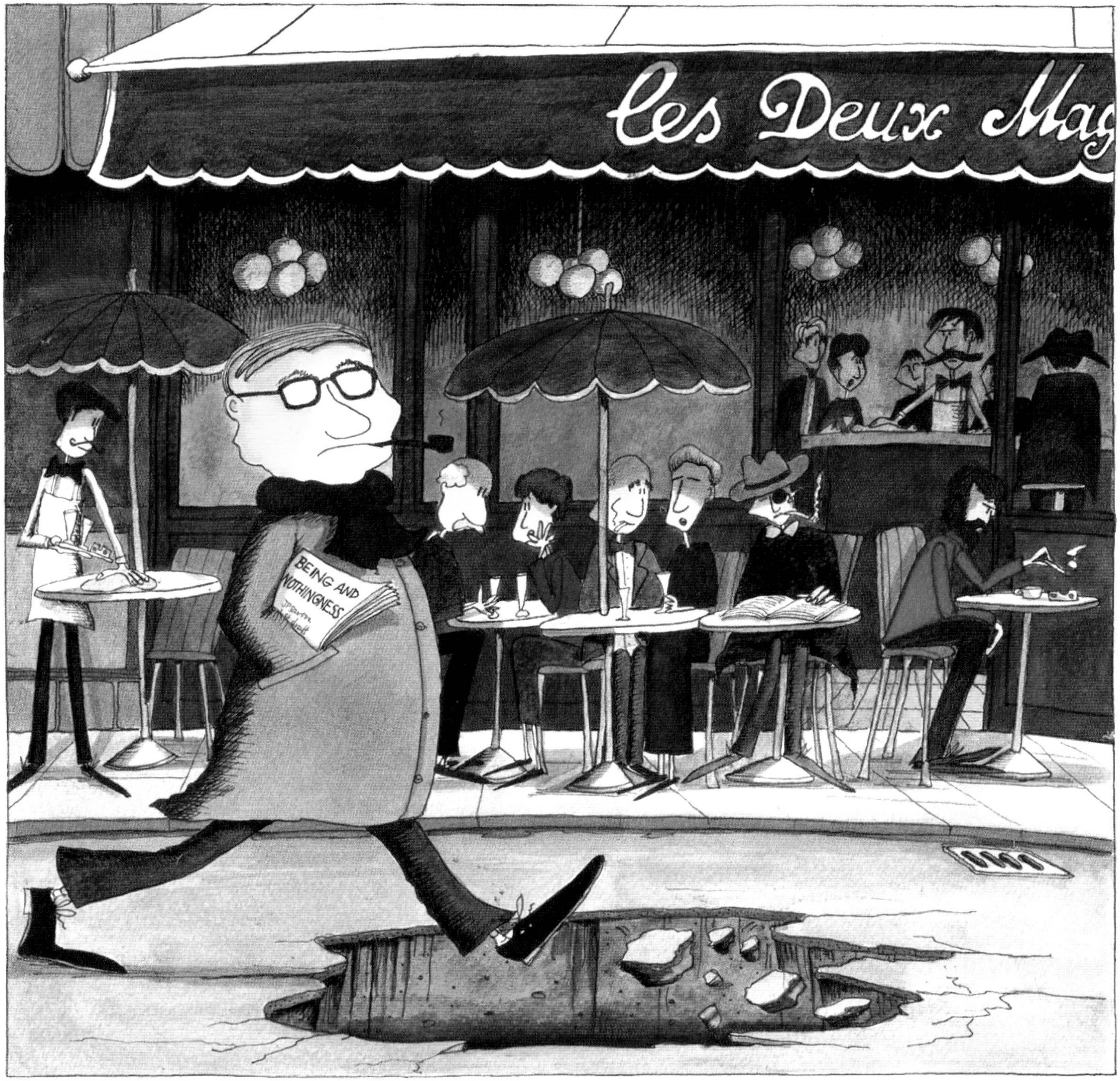
Les Deux Mag
BEING AND NOTHINGNESS

Jean-Paul Sartre goes for a walk.

How was your day?

In April 1902 in Saint-Pierre, Martinique, another quiet day dawned. People went about their business and didn't pay much attention to the rumbling and hissing noise coming from Mount Pelée.

A couple of weeks later though, burning ash began to rain down continuously, and the air stank of sulphur. After their nests were burned up by the lava, a hundred six-foot-long fer-de-lance snakes slithered down the mountain and into town, killing fifty people and hundreds of animals before they were finally themselves killed off by the town's giant street cats. But that wasn't the end of matters.

On 5 May, a landslide of boiling mud spilled into the sea, followed by a tsunami that killed hundreds and, three days later, on 8 May, Mount Pelée finally exploded and completely obliterated Saint-Pierre in an avalanche of lava.

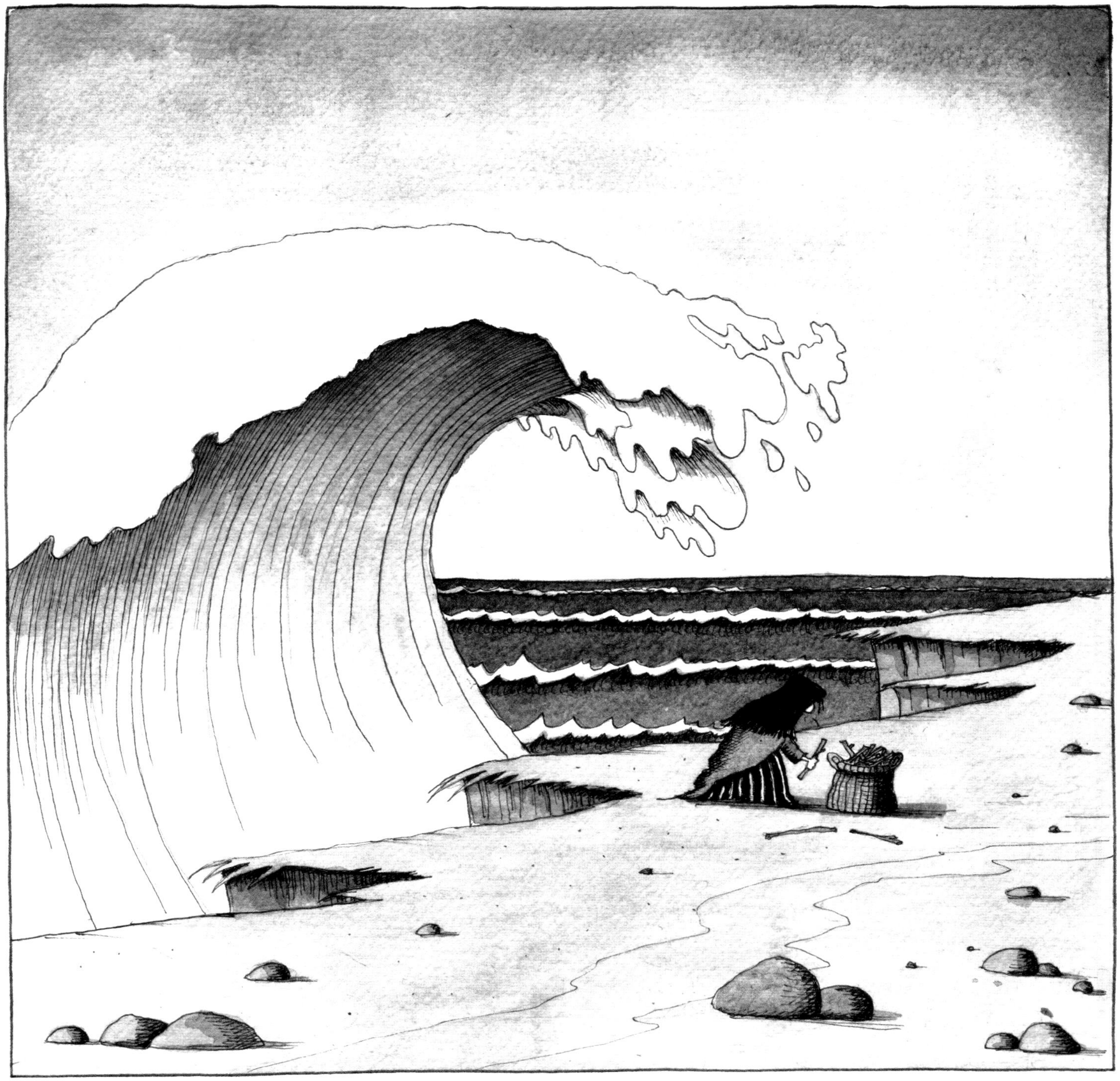

Peig Sayers picks up a few more sticks before going home to finish her famous memoir.

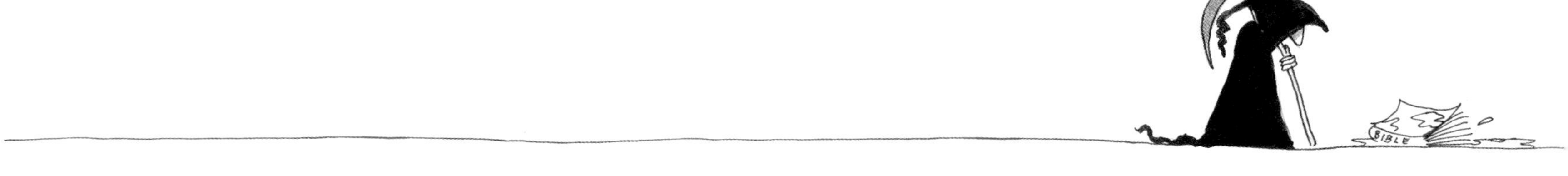
BIBLE

... and also with you

In 1903 a person was beaten to death with a Bible during a healing ceremony gone wrong in Honolulu.

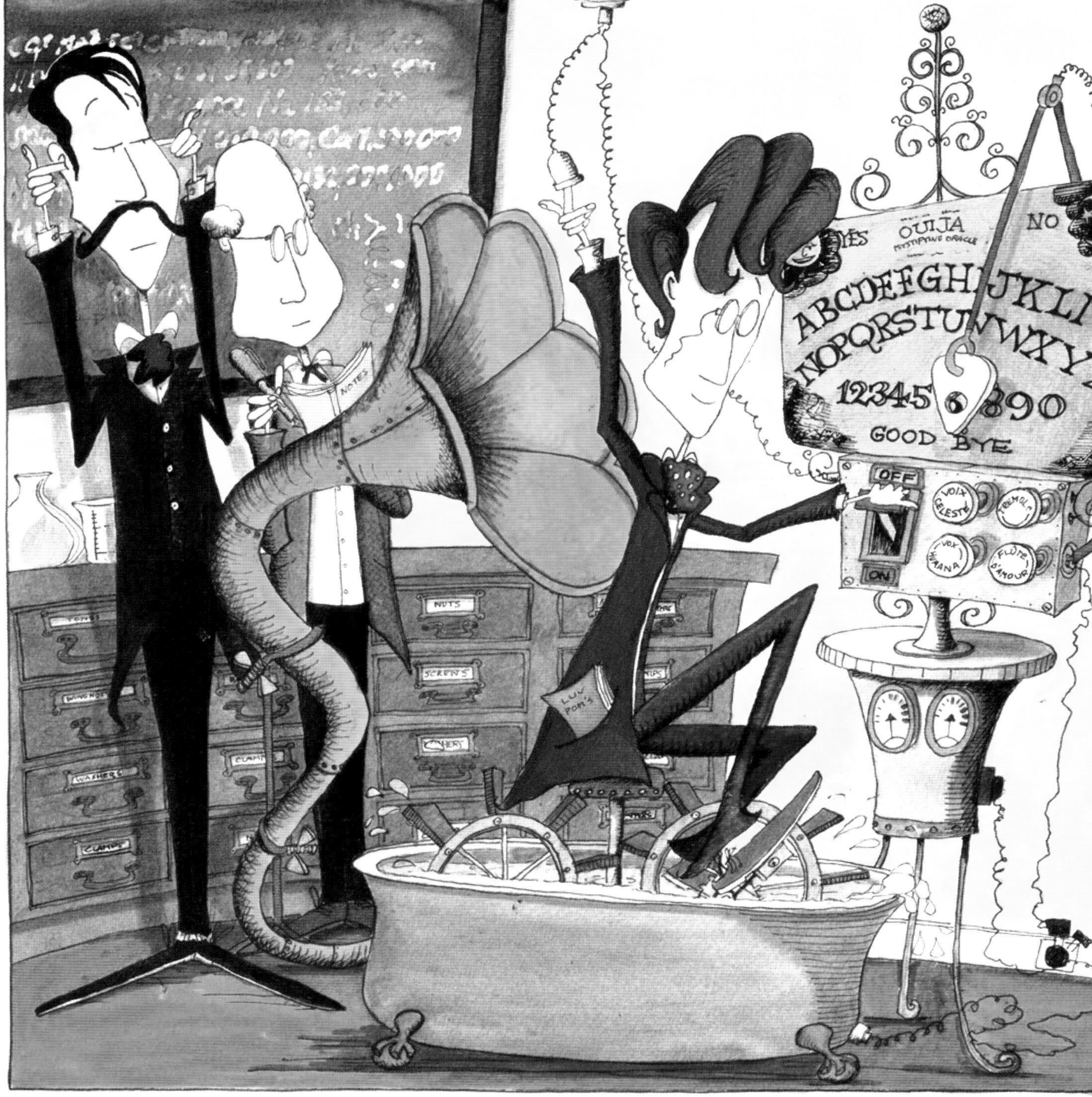
YES
OUIJA
NO
ABCDEFGHIJKLM
NOPQRSTUVWXYZ
GOOD BYE
OFF
ON
VOIX CELESTE
TREMOLO
VOX HUMANA
FLÛTE D'AMOUR
NOTES
NUTS
SCREWS
WASHERS
CLAMPS

An excited WB Yeats makes another scientific attempt to speak to the Dead.

Too much sugar is bad for you

In 1919, citizens living in the North End neighbourhood of Boston, Massachusetts woke to the sound of rumbling followed by a very strong smell of molasses.

A huge molasses storage tank, owned by the Purity Distilling Company, had burst in the industrial quarter, and approximately two million gallons the stuff swept down the streets at an estimated 35 miles an hour, smothering everything in its path. Twenty-one people died and 150 were injured, drowned in a sticky black treacly mess.

For many years afterward, residents claimed that on hot summer days the area still stank of molasses.

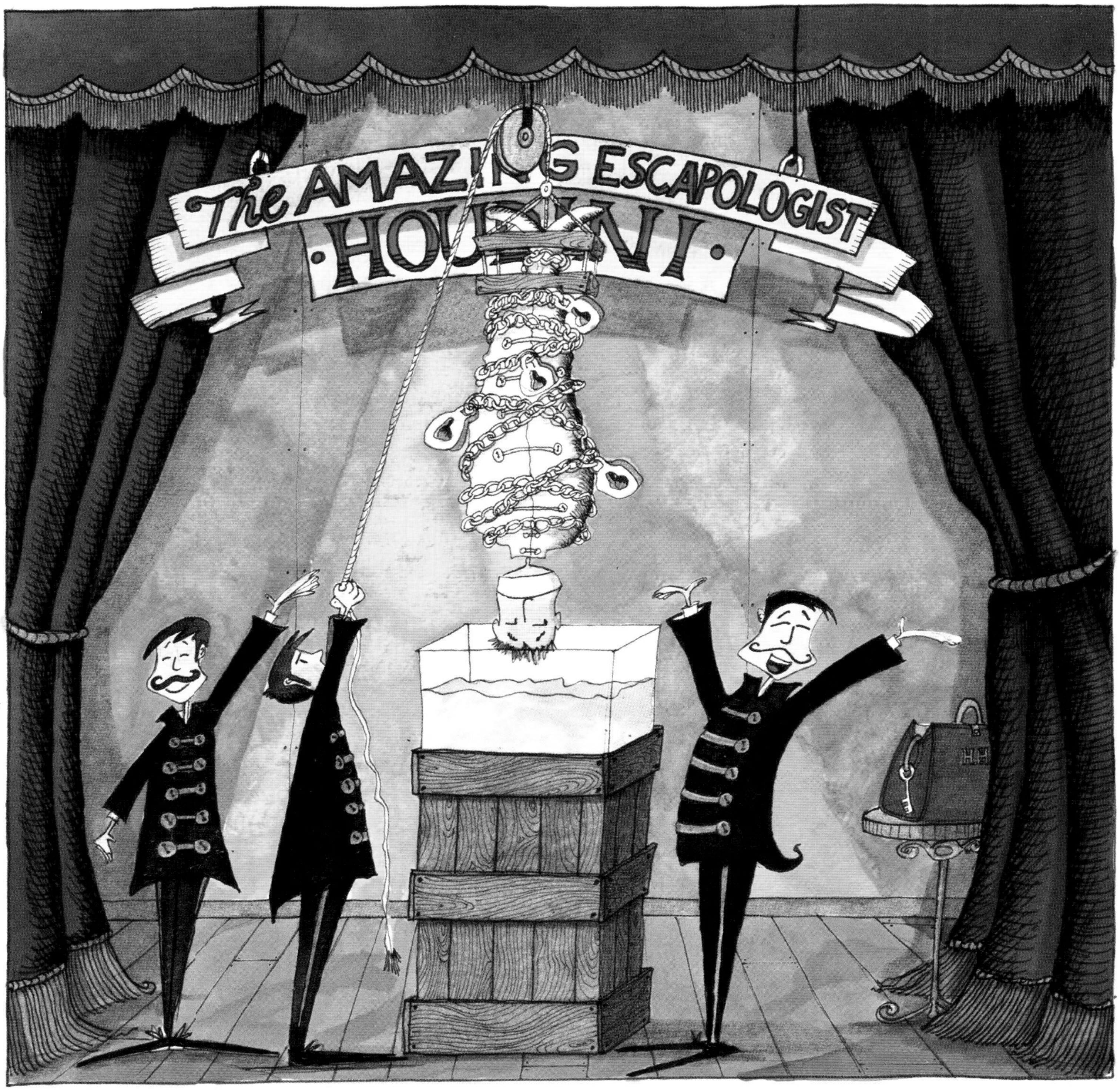
The AMAZI G ESCAPOLOGIST
H.H.

Hell of a time to forget your keys.

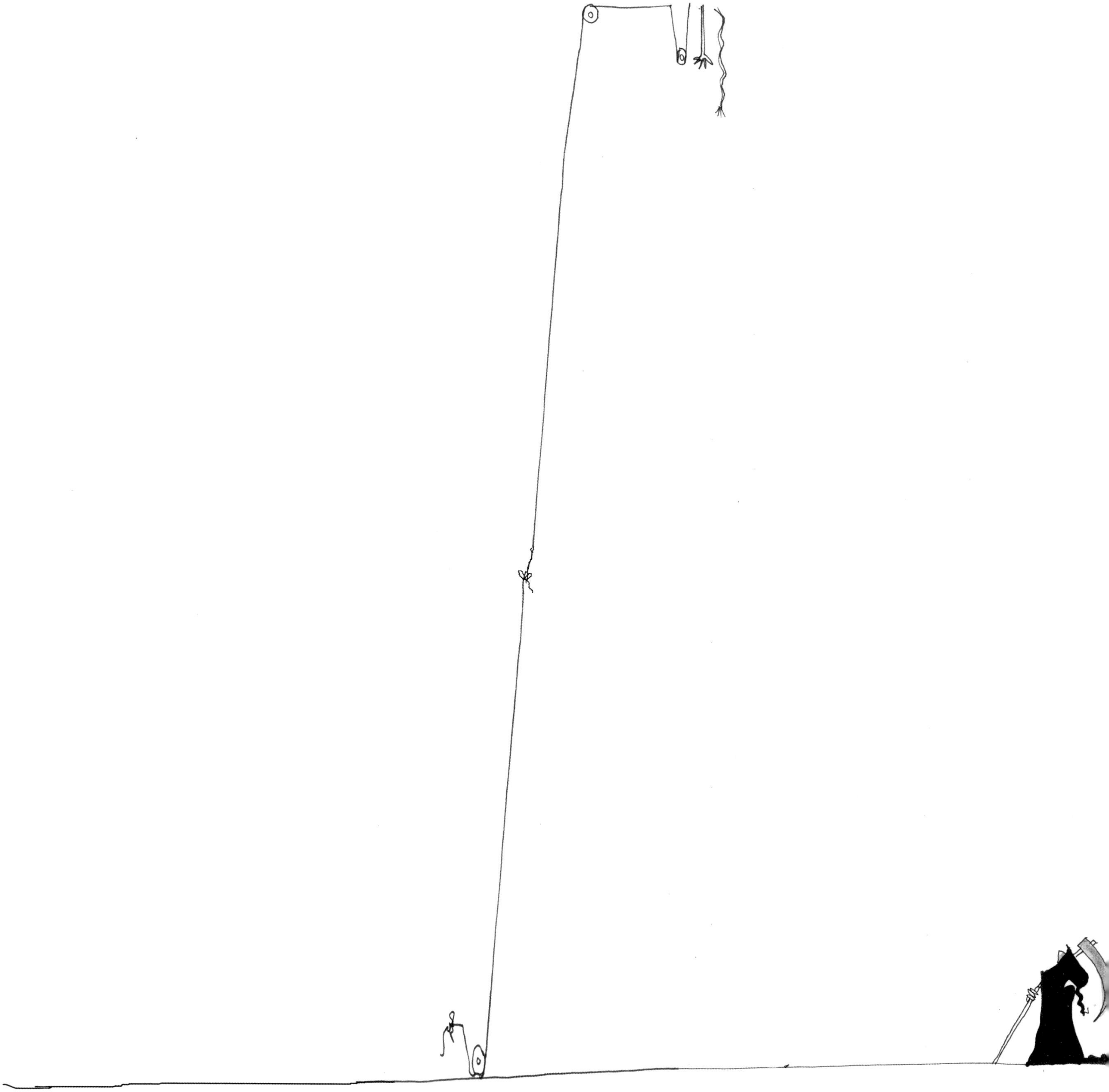

Maybe we could hang out later

Thomas Midgley Jr was an American engineer, chemist and president of the American Chemical Society who invented the tetraethyl lead additive to gasoline and chlorofluorocarbons (otherwise known as CFCs).

Unfortunately, Midgley contracted polio at the age fifty-one and became severely disabled. Undeterred by his disability, he devised an elaborate, W. Heath Robinson-style system of ropes and pulleys to help lift him from bed. One morning, however, he became accidentally entangled in the ropes and died of strangulation in 1944 at the age of fifty-five.

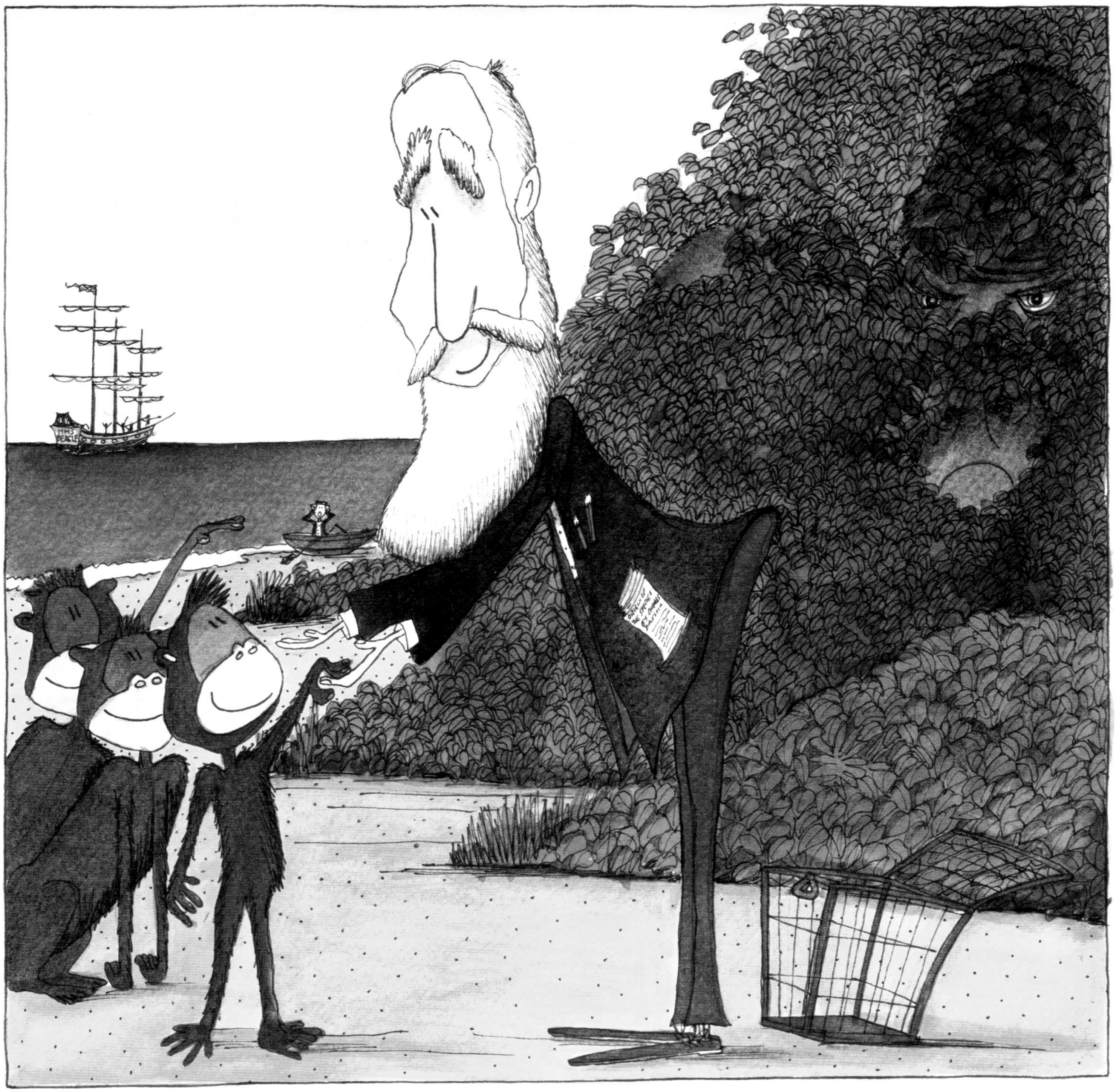

Charles Darwin picks a friendly specimen to bring back to England.

And finally

In 1996, the top Darwin Award went to a Polish farmer, Krystof Azninski.

According to Reuters, Mr Azninski and his friends, while drinking, decided to strip naked and engage in a contest of masculinity. They started by hitting each other over the head with frozen turnips, but when one man cut off his own foot with a chainsaw, Azninski upped the ante by taking the chainsaw to his own neck.

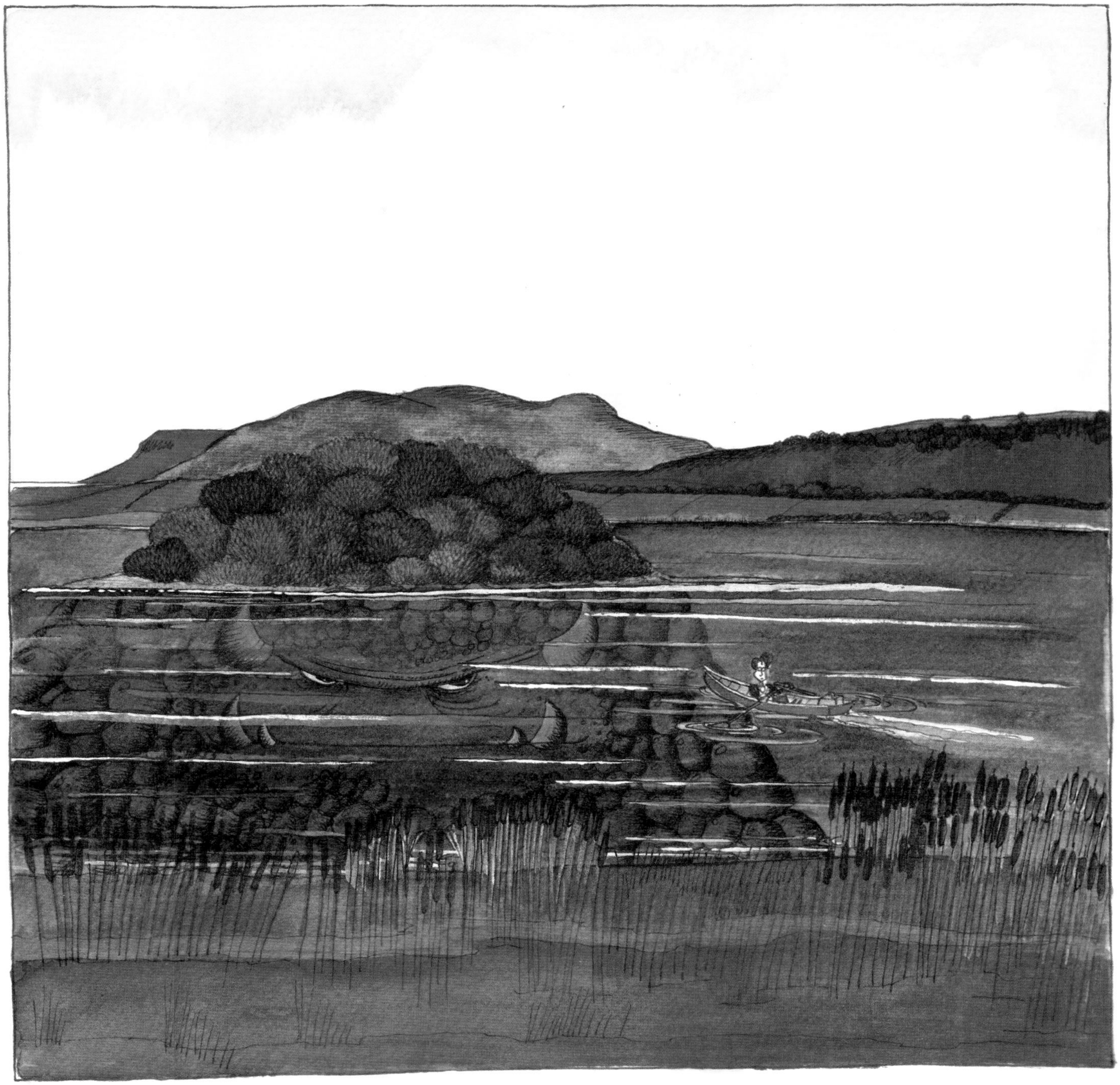

"And I shall find some peace there, for peace comes dropping slow."

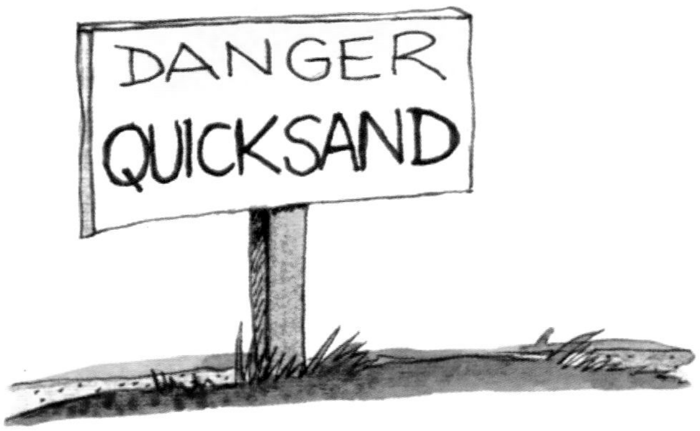
DANGER
QUICKSAND